Annegert Fuchshuber

Carly

Published by The Feminist Press
at The City University of New York
311 E 94th Street, New York, NY 10128-5684

First edition, 1997

Originally published in German as *Karlinchen* by Annette Betz Verlag, an imprint of Verlag Carl Ueberreuter, Vienna/Munich, in 1995.
Published by arrangement with Annette Betz Verlag.

Library of Congress Cataloging-in-Publication Data
Fuchshuber, Annegert.
[Karlinchen. English]
Carly / Annegert Fuchshuber ; translated by Florence Howe and Heidi Kirk. – 1st ed.
p. cm.
Summary: A homeless girl wanders the land searching for food and shelter, but no one will help her until she meets a Fool, who is kinder than all the others.
ISBN 1-55861-177-0 (alk. paper)
[1. Homeless persons–Fiction. 2. Prejudices–Fiction. 3. Kindness–Fiction.] I. Howe, Florence. II. Kirk, Heidi. III. Title.
PZ7.F94CAr 1997
[E]–dc21
97-10799
CIP
AC

The Feminist Press would like to thank Helene Goldfarb, Joanne Markell, Caroline Urvater, and Genevieve Vaughan for their generosity in supporting this publication.

Cover and interior illustration and layout by Annegert Fuchshuber
English-language text design by Dayna Navaro

Printed on acid-free paper

Printed in Austria

03 02 01 00 99 98 97 5 4 3 2 1

CARLY

Annegert Fuchshuber

Translated by Florence Howe and Heidi Kirk

THE FEMINIST PRESS
at The City University of New York
New York

Carly ran away
because fire fell from the sky, and she was hungry,
and no one cared about a child
who was alone and terrified.

Carly ran and ran and did not stop until
she came to a quiet, peaceful village.
Two people sat on a bench in warm sunlight before a house
and talked a little and seemed contented.
Carly asked if she might live there in the village.
And perhaps they also had a little piece of bread
or something else she could eat.

"This is not right!" said one of the villagers.
"A child who wanders about and begs for food!
Someone must do something about this! She belongs in an orphanage!"
They called the police
so that they might catch Carly. But Carly ran away.

Carly came to a forest where she found a few berries
that made her feel a little less hungry.
And on some moss she made a soft, warm bed.
But she still needed more to eat,
and the night noises in the forest frightened her.

No, she could not live there forever,
all alone. So Carly wandered again through the woods,
following her nose until she reached the other side.
There she entered the land of the Stone-eaters.
They were very friendly and gave Carly
a handful of stones to eat, but she couldn't eat stones.
So the Stone-eaters grew very angry.
"Isn't this place good enough for you? If you won't eat
what we have to give you, then you may as well leave!"
Then Carly thought sadly, "They don't like me
because I'm strange and different from them."
And that was true. The Stone-eaters left her standing there.
So Carly walked away.

Again she walked through a huge, dark forest.
Ahead lay the land of the Silk-tails.
"Welcome! Welcome!" they called, and asked
what she would like.
"Oh, just a small piece of bread
and somewhere warm to sleep," said Carly.
"That you can have," twittered the Silk-tails,
"that you can have!"
But then one of them, standing behind Carly, said
in a frightened voice, "It doesn't have a tail!"
Now they all wanted to see Carly from behind,
and when they saw that she really had no tail,
they said, worried, "No, you cannot stay with us.
After all, you don't have a silk-tail."
"But that doesn't matter," Carly tried to comfort them.
"I can hang one around me,
or attach one to me with a safety pin."
"No, no, that won't do," cried the Silk-tails, horrified.
"That won't do at all. For only Silk-tails
are allowed to live in our country."
Carly pleaded and begged, but she had to leave again,
even though it was nighttime, dark, and cold.
Carly thought sadly, "They won't help me
because I'm strange and different from them."

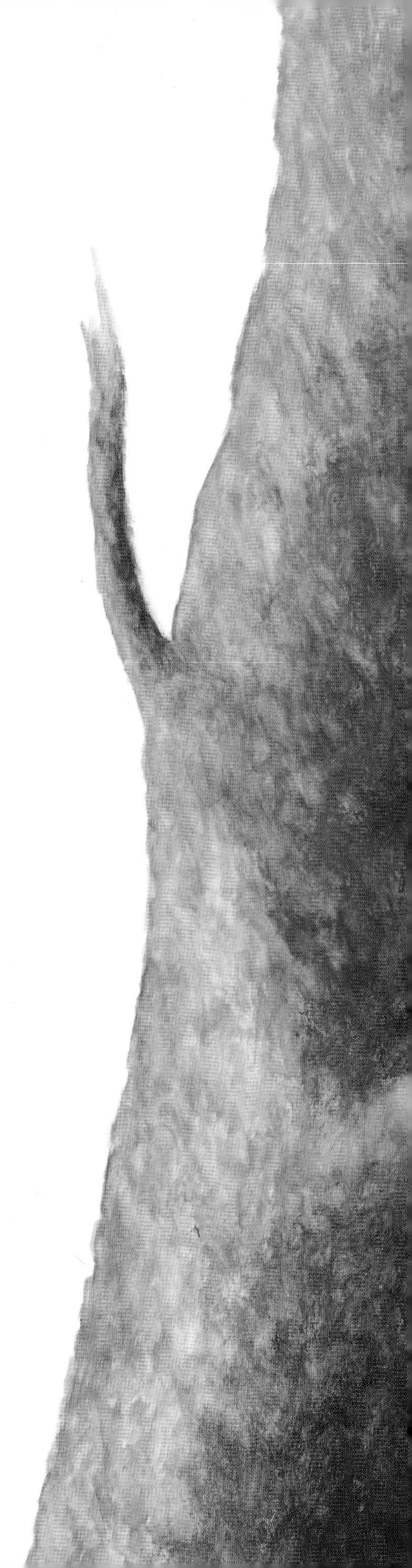

Once again she crossed a large, dark forest.
She came into the land of the Smoky-crows.
Here Carly was greeted warmly.
One Smoky-crow offered her a soft nest, high up
in a bare tree, and a dead mouse to eat,
that already smelled a bit,
which made it especially delicious.
Carly couldn't climb the tree, for it was very tall.
"You must fly up," advised the Smoky-crows.
But Carly couldn't fly.
She didn't want to eat the mouse.
It made her feel sick to her stomach.
"We don't have anything else,"
the Smoky-crows said sadly.
So Carly thought, "They don't understand me
because I am strange and different from them."
There was nothing else to do but move on again.

Once more, she walked through a huge, dark forest.
Then she entered the land of the Greedy-managers.
They were rich and lived in large, comfortable houses
and always had enough to eat.
Whatever food was left over, they threw away.
Even their pets enjoyed nothing but the best food.

When people met in the street,
they hugged and gave each other two kisses,
one on each cheek.
But no one hugged Carly,
though her hunger and loneliness were
as clear as the nose on her face.
Shyly, she greeted two people and asked for something to eat
and a warm place to sleep. But that request angered them!
"Beat it! We have nothing to spare!"
the Greedy-managers shouted.

BER
ex
F
ALA
R·7932

SI'
GARA
FLY
BUB
SR
156217

"Rich people don't know how much hunger hurts,"
Carly thought. "I must look for poor people.
They know how painful it is when no one will help you."
She walked to the edge of the city,
behind the big factories and the garbage dump.
There poor people lived in small shacks.
"Go away!" they shouted, when they saw the strange child.
"We've no use for you here. The boat is full."
"But I don't see any boat," said Carly, astonished.
"When a boat is too full, it sinks,"
said the poor people. "When too many poor people live here,
there isn't enough food or space to go around.
Then we all go under."
So Carly understood that she could not stay there.

But she didn't know where else she should go.
And to add to her troubles, it began to rain.

Carly walked out of the city and across the fields.
She saw a huge tree. In its branches
someone had built a house out of junk.
A man sat at the window, looking out
and eating a big cheese sandwich.
"Come here and take a bite of my cheese sandwich,"
he called. "You look hungry and tired.
Rest here where it's dry and warm."
"Who are you?" asked Carly and stared, amazed,
at the man dressed as colorfully and oddly
as his strange house.
"A Fool," he said. "Can't you tell from my clothes?"
"Oh," said Carly, who had never heard of a Fool.
"Is that what people are called who are kind to others?
I have been looking for you for a very long time.
If you will let me, I would like to become a Fool like you."

J F F951c

Fuchshuber, Annegert.

Carly

DATE	ISSUED TO